A Butterfly Called Hope

by *NY Times* best-selling author
Mary Alice Monroe
with *Linda Love*
photography by *Barbara J. Bergwerf*

In my mother's garden there are many flowers: pink, blue, yellow and orange.

They open their petals to the sun.

I call them flying flowers.

monarch   cloudless sulphur   gulf fritillary   black swallowtail

I look at a green milkweed leaf and see a bright yellow and black bug staring back at me.

Chewing . . . chewing . . . chewing.

"Mommy, come quick! What is it? Will it bite me? Or sting me? Will it make me sick?"

"Don't be afraid," my mother says. "It won't hurt you. That is a caterpillar. Someday it will grow to be a beautiful butterfly."

"What kind of butterfly will it be?" I ask, still afraid.

My mother says, "Let's take the caterpillar to Nana Butterfly. She will know."

We place the caterpillar gently on a leaf in a big glass jar. I carry it in my lap in my mother's car.

Nana Butterfly looks in the jar. "You have a monarch caterpillar. You can leave it with me. I'll take good care of it and set the butterfly free."

"No," I tell her, because I love my caterpillar.

"I want to keep it. Mommy, can I please?"

Each morning I put clean paper towels on the bottom of the aquarium and add fresh milkweed from the garden.

Through the glass I can watch my caterpillar getting bigger and bigger.

All day it eats and grows and poops! Caterpillar poop is called *frass*.

I make sure my caterpillar has plenty of fresh milkweed to eat.

One day I do not see the caterpillar eating. I do not see it crawling. I do not see it at all.

"Mommy, come quick! Where is it?"

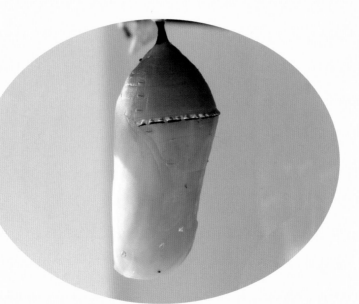

My mother points to a jade green chrysalis hanging at the top of the tank. She tells me, "The change is beginning!"

Eight days later, I see the chrysalis is now black.

"Mommy, come quick! What happened to my chrysalis? Is it sick?"

Mommy says, "Don't worry little one. Your butterfly is almost here. Come and look very closely. You can see the butterfly's wing!"

We watch . . . and wait . . .

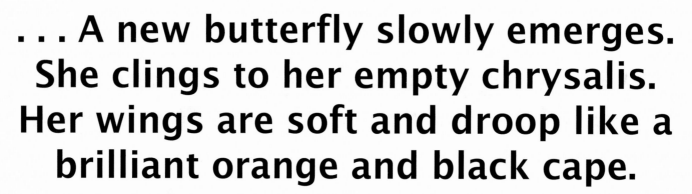

. . . A new butterfly slowly emerges. She clings to her empty chrysalis. Her wings are soft and droop like a brilliant orange and black cape.

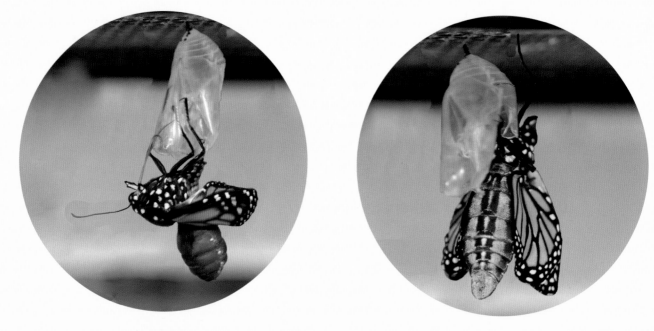

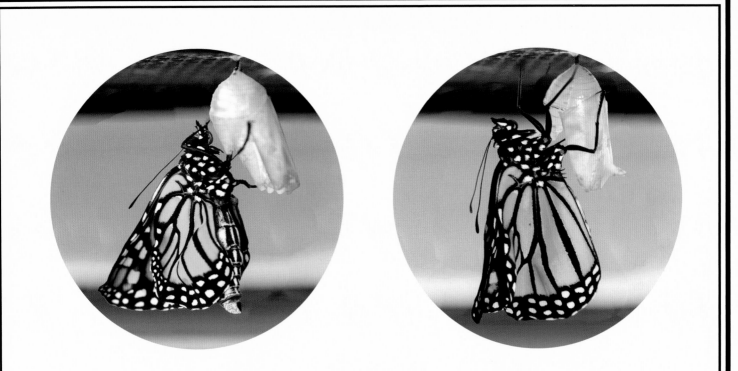

We watch her velvety wings slowly grow larger and larger. When she is ready, she tests them, fluttering one . . . two . . . three times.

My mother says, "It's time for her to fly!"

"No," I cry. "I want to keep my butterfly!"

"A butterfly needs to fly free to sip sweet nectar from flowers. She will lay eggs on milkweed leaves so there will be more butterflies."

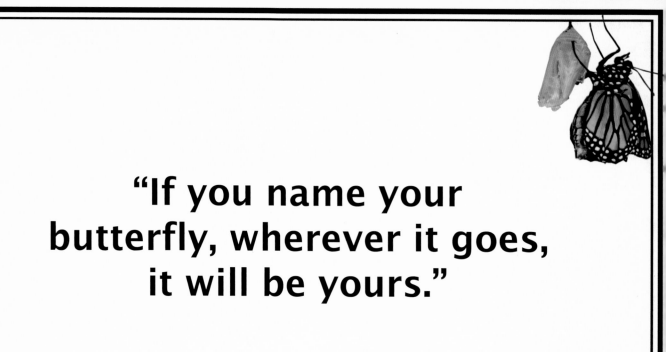

"If you name your
butterfly, wherever it goes,
it will be yours."

"Can I give the butterfly *my*
name?" I ask.

My mother smiles. "Yes, I think
your name is perfect."

My monarch opens her wings to the sun, fluttering in joy. Then, on a soft breeze, my butterfly flies.

I feel the warm sun on my face as I call out,

"Your name is Hope!"

For Creative Minds

Monarch Life Cycle Sequencing

Put the descriptions of the butterfly life cycle stages in order to match the pictures.

The caterpillar eats and eats.

The chrysalis is complete and green.

The caterpillar hatches (larva stage).

The caterpillar starts to turn into a chrysalis.

The adult butterfly flies away and will lay eggs.

The butterfly starts to emerge from the chrysalis.

The adult lays eggs. Compare the egg size to the dime.

The chrysalis turns clear. We see black butterfly wings.

Answers: 1) Adult lays eggs. 2) The caterpillar hatches. 3) The caterpillar starts to turn into a chrysalis. 5) The green chrysalis is complete. 6) The chrysalis turns clear. 7) The butterfly emerges. 8) The butterfly flies away.

Butterfly Vocabulary Matching Activity

Match the word to the description.

butterfly

chrysalis

egg

frass

host plant

instar

larva

metamorphosis

migration

molt

nectar

proboscis

1. This is the final and adult stage of this insect's life cycle.

2. This is the second stage of the life cycle when the caterpillar is an eating machine and grows. Under normal summer temperatures, this stage lasts from nine to fourteen days.

3. This is the "resting stage" during which a caterpillar changes into a butterfly. This third stage of development lasts ten to fourteen days under normal summer conditions and is also called "pupa."

4. This is laid by an adult female on a milkweed leaf and is the first stage of the life cycle.

5. A special word for caterpillar droppings (poop).

6. The only plants on which butterflies and other insects lay their eggs. Monarchs only use milkweed. There are over 100 types of milkweed. Other butterflies use other plants.

7. This is the time between molts of the caterpillar when the body grows. Monarch caterpillars have five.

8. This is a life-cycle change of an insect to an adult.

9. This journey from one location to another is usually to follow food sources and climate changes.

10. As a caterpillar grows, it sheds its outer layer of skin with a new, bigger skin underneath that will then harden.

11. The sugary juice made by flowers that is used as food by butterflies and other insects.

12. A butterfly uses this straw-like tongue to drink water and nectar. When not in use, the butterfly curls it up and keeps it out of the way.

Answers: 1) Butterfly, 2) Larva, 3) Chrysalis, 4) Egg, 5) Frass, 6) Host Plant, 7) Instar, 8) Metamorphosis, 9) Migration, 10) Molt, 11) Nectar, 12) Proboscis

Monarch Generations and Migrations

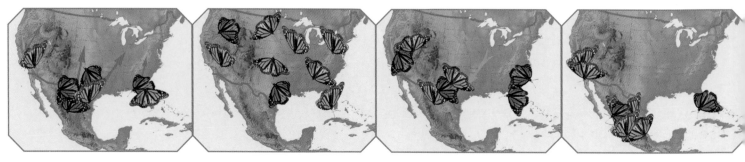

Spring   Summer   Fall   Winter

Most of us are familiar with birds migrating in the spring and fall. Did you know that some insects, like the monarch butterfly, migrate too?

The Generations

The generation that spent the winter in Mexico will fly north to look for milkweed. These monarchs will lay eggs and after a very long life, will die.

First generation—March and April: The eggs hatch into caterpillars, form chrysalises, and emerge as butterflies. These butterflies continue to migrate north to the area around where their parents hatched, laying eggs along the way.

Second generation—May, June and July: The eggs hatch into caterpillars, form chrysalises, and emerge as butterflies.

Third generation—July and August: The eggs hatch into caterpillars, form chrysalises, emerge as butterflies, and then lay their eggs.

Fourth generation—August, September and October: The eggs hatch into caterpillars, form chrysalises, and emerge as butterflies. Depending on the population to which they belong, monarchs migrate south to Southern California or Mexico where it is warm enough for them to survive the winter. Even though these butterflies have never been there before, they somehow find their way and usually even go to the same trees as their great-grandparents! Once there, the butterflies stay through the winter. Monarchs in Florida do not migrate. Some scientists are studying whether some "East Coast" monarchs migrate to Florida instead of Mexico.

Fourth generation (still)—February and March: Monarch butterflies start flying north again and lay their eggs. The cycle starts again!

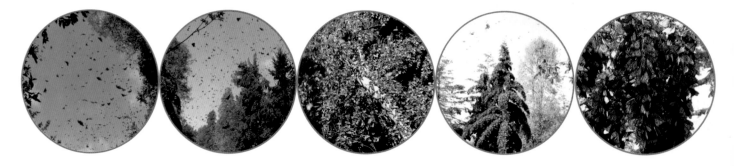

Raising Monarchs

You will need a safe habitat for the caterpillars and lots of fresh milkweed. You should use milkweed that is native to your area. For more detailed information, please go to the "teaching activities" by clicking on the book's cover at SylvanDellPublishing.com.

Caring for the caterpillars:

Monarch caterpillars are very hungry but they *only* eat milkweed leaves! Add leaves to the habitat daily. When the caterpillars get bigger, they will eat a lot, so be sure to check often and add leaves as needed.

Keep the leaves moist by adding water to small containers or wrap the ends in a damp paper towel. If they are not fresh, keep extra milkweed leaves in a plastic bag in the refrigerator.

Keep the habitat clean by removing the frass and dried leaves and changing the paper towels often.

Things to watch for:

If your caterpillar wanders off and stops moving, do not disturb it. It is molting.

Don't let your caterpillars get too crowded or your habitat dirty. Bacteria can form that can make your caterpillars sick.

After 10-14 days, your large caterpillar will stop eating and wander to the top of the habitat. First it will spin a silk knot, then tuck its feet in, and hang head down. It looks like a "J." After about 14 hours, it will begin to twist and do a "pupa dance" as it changes into a pale green chrysalis.

About two weeks later, the chrysalis will look black. This means that your butterfly will emerge in about 24 hours!

Monarchs usually emerge early in the morning—it happens fast so don't miss it! The butterfly will pop out and hang on the chrysalis shell for two hours while it pumps fluid into the wings. You can watch the wings grow. This is a dangerous time for a butterfly. If it falls, or if it is touched, the wings will be damaged and it won't fly. The new butterfly will hang for several hours while the wings dry.

Three to four hours after the butterfly emerges it is safe to release to the garden. The butterfly doesn't eat until the day after it is born, so if it is raining, you can keep your butterfly in a flight cage for a day or two.

Release the butterfly in your garden where there are flowers. If you live in a city, you can release the butterfly in a park or a garden center, but be sure not to release it where people have sprayed pesticides.

Thanks to Karen Oberhauser, Director of Monarchs in the Classroom Program and President of the Monarch Butterfly Sanctuary Foundation; and to Trecia Neal, biologist at the Fernbank Science Center and Monarchs Across Georgia for verifying the accuracy of the information in this book.

Library of Congress Cataloging-in-Publication Data

Monroe, Mary Alice, author.
  A butterfly called Hope / by NY Times best-selling author Mary Alice Monroe, with Linda Love ; photography by Barbara J. Bergwerf.
      pages cm
   Audience: 4-9.
   Audience: K to grade 3.
   ISBN 978-1-60718-854-4 (hardcover English) -- ISBN 978-1-60718-856-8 (pbk. English) -- ISBN 978-1-60718-857-5 (downloadable (pdf) ebook) -- ISBN 978-1-60718-859-9 (interactive web-based ebook) -- ISBN 978-1-60718-858-2 (downloadable (pdf) Spanish ebook)
  1. Monarch butterfly--Juvenile literature. 2. Butterflies--Juvenile literature. 3. Caterpillars--Juvenile literature. 4. Metamorphosis--Juvenile literature. I. Love, Linda, 1944- author. II. Bergwerf, Barbara J., illustrator. III. Title.
   QL561.D3M664 2013
   595.78'9--dc23
                                    2013013641

Translated into Spanish by Rosalyna Toth: Una mariposa llamada Esperanza

Lexile® Level: 430
Educator keywords: butterfly life cycle, metamorphosis

Manufactured in China, June 2013
This product conforms to CPSIA 2008
First Printing

Sylvan Dell Publishing
Mt. Pleasant, SC 29464
www.SylvanDellPublishing.com